A WOLF at the DOOR!

Nick Ward

Albury Books

For Simon,
for all his help

N.W.

Published by Albury Books in 2022
Albury Court, Albury, Thame,
OX9 2LP, United Kingdom

Text © Nick Ward • Illustrations © Nick Ward
The rights of Nick Ward to be identified as the author and illustrator have been asserted by
them in accordance with the Copyright, Designs and Patents Act, 1988

ISBN 978-1-910235-17-1 (paperback)

A CIP catalogue record for this
book is available from the British Library
10 9 8 7 6 5 4 3 2 1
Printed in China

One quiet afternoon, while Father Bear
was in the yard chopping wood, Little Bear
sat reading his favorite book.
All was cosy and peaceful, when ...

Knock! Knock! went the door.
"Who's there?" asked Little Bear,
jumping down from his chair.

"It's Billy," a tiny voice bleated. "Please let me in."
Little Bear lifted the latch,
opened the door and in trotted ...

... Little Billy Goat Gruff!
"Lock the door, quickly,"
bleated Billy.
"A wolf is after me!
And he shouted,
'Come out, come out,
wherever you are!'"

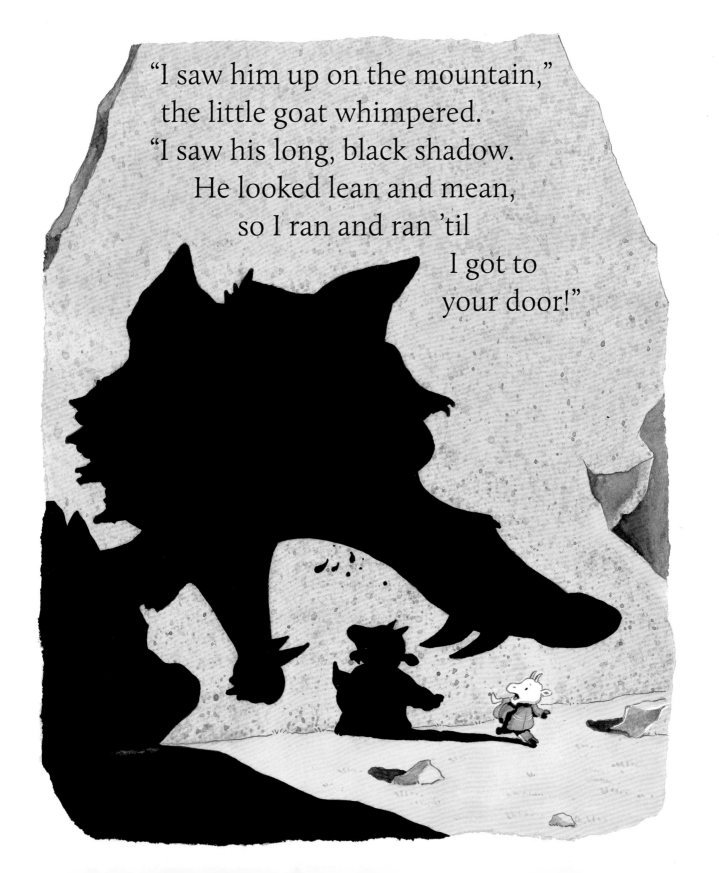

"I saw him up on the mountain,"
the little goat whimpered.
"I saw his long, black shadow.
He looked lean and mean,
so I ran and ran 'til
I got to
your door!"

Little Bear sat Billy down.
"Don't worry," he said. "You're safe here."
And he started to read Billy a story.
All was cosy and quiet, when ...

KNOCK KNOCK!

went the door!
"Who's there?" called Little Bear.
"It's the Squealer Boys!
Please let us in."

Little Bear lifted the latch,
opened the door, and in trotted ...

... the three little pigs!
"Lock the door, quickly!" they cried.
"A huge wolf is after us!
He came to our house and he roared,
'Come out, come out, wherever you are!'
He was fierce. He was angry!"
"And he was lean and mean,"
added Billy.

"We left our house and ran
and ran, 'til we got to your
door," squealed
the three pigs.

Little Bear let
them in and
locked the door.

"Don't worry," said Little Bear.
"You're safe here."
And he sat them down to listen to the story.
All was quiet and calm, when ...

KNOCK KNOCK! went the door!
"Who's there?" called Little Bear.
"It's Bo," said a voice.
"Please let me in."

Little Bear lifted
the latch, opened
the door and
in rushed ...

... Little Bo Peep and all
her sheep!
"Lock the door," cried Bo Peep.
"A wolf is after us!"
"What happened?"
asked Little Bear, as he
locked the door, quickly.

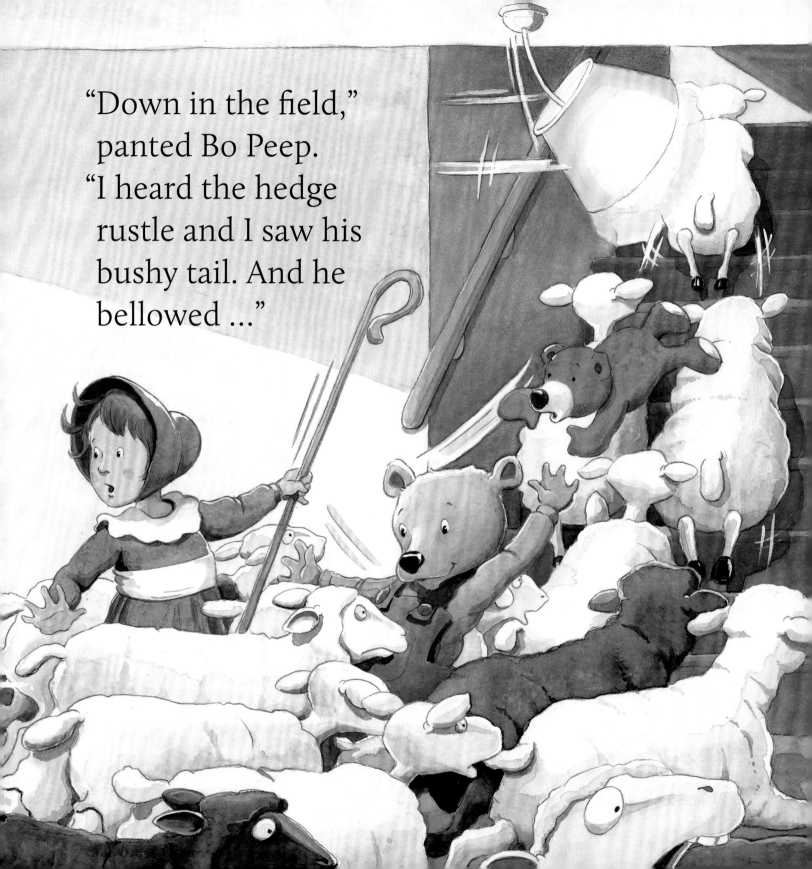

"Down in the field," panted Bo Peep. "I heard the hedge rustle and I saw his bushy tail. And he bellowed ..."

"We ran for our lives," chorused the sheep.
"But he chased us!"
"We could hear him panting."
"We could feel his hot wolfie breath."
"He was huge," baaed the sheep.
"He was fierce and angry," piped the pigs.
"He was lean and mean," bleated Billy.
"And we didn't stop 'til we got to your door,"
  finished Bo Peep.

So Little Bear sat them all down and
started to read his story.
But he kept being interrupted by a
Knock! Knock! at the door.

First there
was Little
Red Riding
Hood,

then
Cinderella,

and finally
Goldilocks.

They had all come to hide
from the wicked wolf.
"Don't worry," Little Bear told them.
"You are all safe here."

Father Bear came in from the yard. "Goodness," he gasped. "What are all your friends doing here?"

"They've escaped from a terrible wolf," said Little Bear.

Just then, **KNOCK KNOCK!** went the door. The house ... went ... very ... very ... quiet.

Father Bear slowly
unlocked the door.
"Who's there?" he boomed...

They all went out and played 'til bedtime! "That was fun," said Wolfie afterwards.
"Come again soon!" said Little Bear.
"Oh, yes!" cried Wolfie, excitedly.
"And tomorrow I'll bring my big brother!"